Lucky saves the Circus

By: Brian Stewart

BOOK WRITING
PIONEER

Preface
(from the Author)
Welcome, to the, Lucky Big Adventure Series
Thank you for your purchase. This book was written to help young children and their parents or readers to have talking points and situations to discuss acceptance. Every character in this story has a function in life, their own passion, hopes, and dreams. At the end of each page, there is an opportunity to discuss and learn about acceptance of others and their own personnel needs. We all have gifts we like to share with others, but we all have our own needs and desires. Understanding and accepting others for who and what they are is a learned behavior.
Again, Thank you
Brian Stewart

Lucky Big Adventure Books:

Lucky Gets A Pony
Lucky Saves The Circus
Lucky Goes To The Derby
Lucky Saves Christmas
Lucky Learns To Skate

LUCKY TOLD TONY THE PONY.
CHEER UP! THE CIRCUS
HAS COME TO TOWN.

THEY HAVE CAMELS TO RIDE OR A TRAIN
FULL OF TROLLS. DRIVEN BY A CLOWN.
I'LL COLLECT THE MONEY. YOU GIVE THEM RID
GINGER CAN LEAD YOU AROUND.
CIRCUS

MR. RINGMASTER. MY NAME IS LUCKY, AND I'VE GOT A DEAL FOR YOU.
LEASE DON'T ANSWER OR SAY ANYTHING, JUST WAIT UNTIL I GET THROUGH.
I WILL RENT YOU OUR TONY THE PONY. AND WE GET JUST HALF HIS DUE,
THE RINGMASTER SAID OKAY LUCKY. I WILL MAKE THAT DEAL WITH YOU.

HE PUT US IN THE CENTER RING, CHILDREN START TO CHEER AND JUMP,
CAMEL RIDES WERE IN THE OTHER RING, BUT THEY ONLY HAD ONE HUMP.
RIDE TONY THE PONY, FOR ONLY TEN DOLLARS, TWO LAPS AROUND THE RING,
FORM A LINE RIGHT HERE, HEY GINGER, TREAT EACH RIDER, LIKE THEY ARE KING.

LADIES AND GENTLEMEN. BOYS AND GIRLS.
ARE YOU READY TO START THIS SHOW?
EVERYONE CLEARED THE FLOOR. AND
INTO THE RINGS. THE JUGGLERS. THEY DID GO.

THE JUGGLERS TOSSED RINGS WAY UP HIGH,
THEN CAUGHT THEM VERY WELL,
THEY TOSSED BOWLING PINS, FEDORAS, AND BATONS
WHICH MADE EVERYBODY YELL.

THEN CAME THE DANCING CAMELS AND
THEIR FUNNY LITTLE LLAMA FRIENDS.
THEY DANCED TO THE MUSIC, TONY THE PONY.
WANTED TO SEE THAT AGAIN.

THEN CAME FOUR DANCING HORSES:
THEY DANCED WITH LOTS OF PRIDE.
THEY TROTTED AND CANTERED AROUND
THE RING, ALL WITHOUT A RIDE.

OUT CAME THE LADY ACROBATS, THEIR ROPES
THEY WRAPPED AROUND.
THEY LET THE ROPES UNRAVEL AND
DESCENDED TO THE GROUND.

THEN CAME A CONTORTIONIST ACROBAT.
DOING YOGA WITHOUT A CHAIR.
HE WAS WRAPPED AROUND HIMSELF
AND TWENTY FEET UP IN THE AIR.
HE ALMOST FELL WHEN HE DID A HANDSTAND AND
GAVE THE CROWD A SCARE.
GINGER THOUGHT IT WAS AMAZING.
BUT I WOULDN'T TRY IT. NOT EVEN ON A DARE.
I WOULDN'T DO A HANDSTAND ON A POLE.
TWENTY FEET UP IN THE AIR.

NOW IT'S INTERMISSION, POPCORN, AND LEMONADE,
IT'S TIME TO GET A LITTLE TREAT.
DO YOU WANT FUNNEL CAKE OR COTTON CANDY?
I THINK I WANT SOMETHING SWEET.
THERE'S CORN DOGS AND SNOW CONES,
PLENTY OF SOUVENIRS, AND PLENTY TO EAT.
SOUVENIR BLOW_UP TOYS, GLOW IN THE DARK FACE PAINTING,
NOW THAT WAS PRETTY NEAT.

THEN CAME THE FLYING SAMURAI, CATAPULTING WAY UP HIG
UP IN THE AIR AND LANDING ON ANOTHER GUY.
THEN EIGHT OF THE NARIO BROTHERS. WITH A LONG JUMP RO
THEY RAN IN. OUT. UP AND DOWN. JUMPING FROM A SLOPE

THE CROWD WAS GETTING RESTLESS:
EXCITEMENT WAS STARTING TO STRAY.
THEY WANTED FREDO THE MAGNIFICENT
FOR HE IS WHY THEY PAY.

THEY CAME TO SEE FREDO THE MAGNIFICENT.
HE WALKED THE TIGHTROPE WAY UP THERE.
HE'S NOT PERFORMING TONIGHT. TRIPPED ON TH
CAMELS TOE. AND TORE HIS KNEE, UPON A CHAI

THE RINGMASTER ASKED LUCKY, DOES TONY THE PONY, DO ANY TRICKS?
I NEED ONE OR TWO MORE ACTS, CAUSE THIS CIRCUS WE'VE GOT TO FIX.
TONY THE PONY KNOWS MANY TRICKS: HE CAN EVEN DO THE MOON WALK,
PLAY SOMETHING BY MICHAEL JACKSON. THEY'LL ALL GO HOME AND TALK.

THEY REALLY LOVED HIS DANCING, AND THEY LOVED TO WATCH HIM BOW
WELL, THEY WATCHED TONY THE PONY PERFORM, THEN HE TOOK THIS VO

UCKY, YOU HAVE GOT TO SAVE THIS CIRCUS.
I'M GOING TO TELL YOU HOW.
YOU BETTER GET UP ON THAT HIGH WIRE.
YOU BETTER GET UP THERE NOW.

LADIES AND GENTLEMEN. GIVE YOUR ATTENTION WAY UP HIGH.
LUCKY. THE MAGNIFICENT ON THE PLATFORM. IS ABOUT TO FLY.
HE GRABBED THE BAR AND SWUNG WITH SUCH GRACE.
SPUN UP IN THE AIR AND CAME DOWN ABOUT FACE.

HE WAS SWINGING FROM BAR TO BAR, UP IN THE AIR HE FLEW.
THEN, LANDED ON THE HIGH WIRE: NOW, THAT MOVE WAS NEW.
HE WAS WOBBLING ON THE TIGHTROPE, FROM
THE CROWD, THE TENSION GREW.
HE ROSE UP ON HIS TIPSY TOES, AND AWAY HE FLEW.

WHEN HE REACHED THE OTHER END, HE GRABBED A STABLE POL
HE FIRST TOOK A BOW FOR THE CROWD, THEN SLID DOWN BELO
MR. RINGMASTER, WE SAVED YOUR CIRCUS: NOW WE HAVE TO G

THEN LUCKY, HIS FRIEND GINGER, AND TONY THE PONY WALKED AWAY.
WELL, THEY SAVED THE CIRCUS: THEY REALLY EARNED THEIR PAY.
LUCKY TOLD GINGER, GO HOME AND PRACTICE YOUR GUITAR TODAY.
I'LL PUT TONY THE PONY IN THE BARN AND GIVE HIM SOME EXTRA HAY.
TOMORROW IS A NEW ADVENTURE... OR MAYBE JUST ANOTHER DAY!